The Runaway Bed

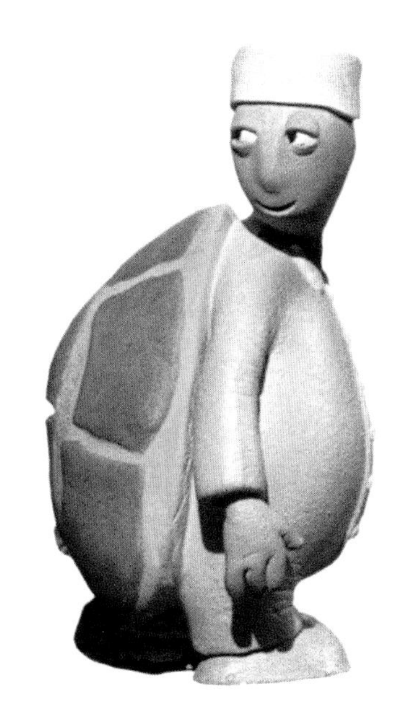

Nicholas Allan

RED FOX

A Red Fox Book

Published by Random House Children's Books
20 Vauxhall Bridge Road, London SW1V 2SA

A division of The Random House Group Ltd
London Melbourne Sydney Auckland
Johannesburg and agencies throughout the world

1 3 5 7 9 10 8 6 4 2

Printed and bound in Italy by Lego SPA

THE RANDOM HOUSE GROUP Limited Reg. No. 954009

ISBN 0 09 940465 6

It was charity week at Hilltop Hospital.

Everyone was busy: Arthur was putting up balloons, Surgeon Sally was preparing for the wheelchair race, and Dr Matthews was selling his joke book.

Suddenly there was the sound of a siren, and the ambulance arrived.

'Must be an emergency!' said Surgeon Sally, as the two Teds opened the back of the ambulance and pulled out a stretcher.

'Only me!' A sleepy tortoise sat up.

'Dr Atticus! Are you ill?' asked Dr Matthews.

'No, no. I'm pretending to be a patient today for charity. So I thought I'd ask the Teds to collect me.'

'Well, really!' complained Sally. 'What a waste of hospital time. You must be The Laziest Doctor in the World.'

'I can't help it. It's just the way I am,' said Dr Atticus, and fell asleep again.

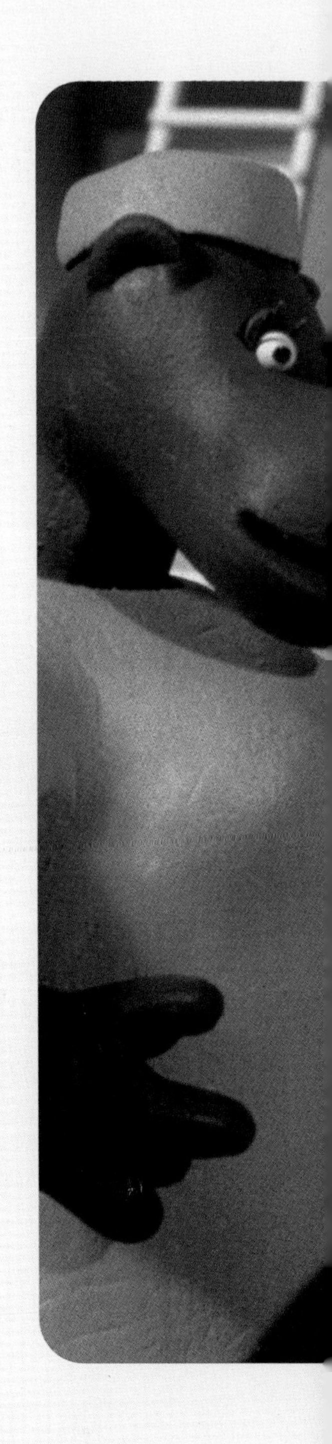

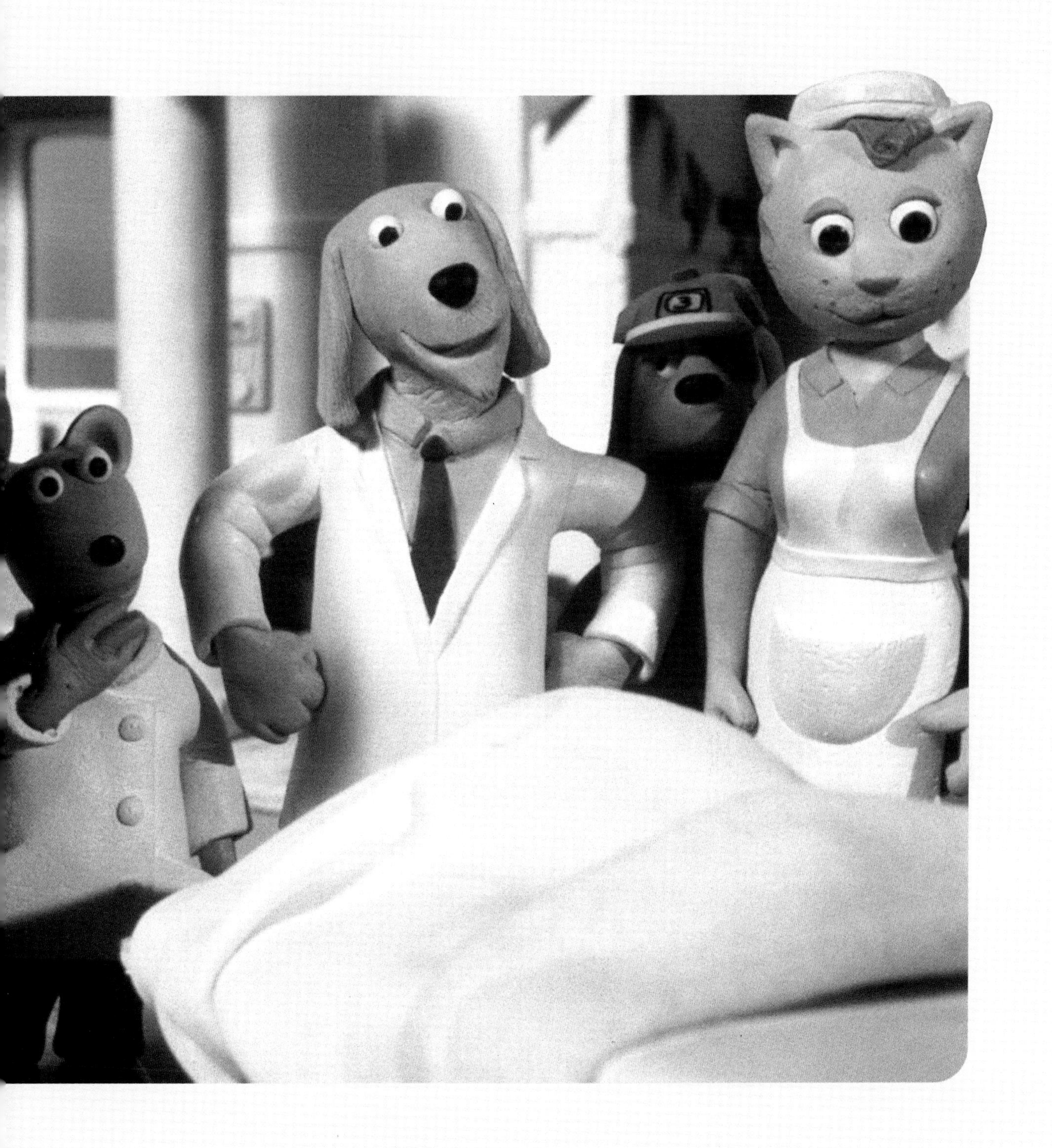

A little later, Dr Atticus's alarm clock rang.

'Ooh, must be lunch time. Nurse! Where's my lunch?'

'You're not a real patient, Dr Atticus,' said Nurse Kitty. 'You can get your own lunch.'

'If I'm pretending to be a patient I want to do it properly. Five lettuce leaves, please. A carrot. Oh, and a cool glass of cabbage juice.'

Nurse Kitty went off to the kitchen... and that's when it happened.

While Dr Atticus was rattling the collection box, he fell asleep again. The box rolled off the bed... and released the break pedal.

'Here's your lunch,' Nurse Kitty said, returning. But by then Dr Atticus and the bed had disappeared.

Dr Atticus was having pleasant dreams about cabbage as he and the bed sped out of the hospital and down the hill. At the bottom of the hill was a pond, and by the pond, Derek Duck was fishing.

'Aarrgh!' cried Derek, as the bed hit him.

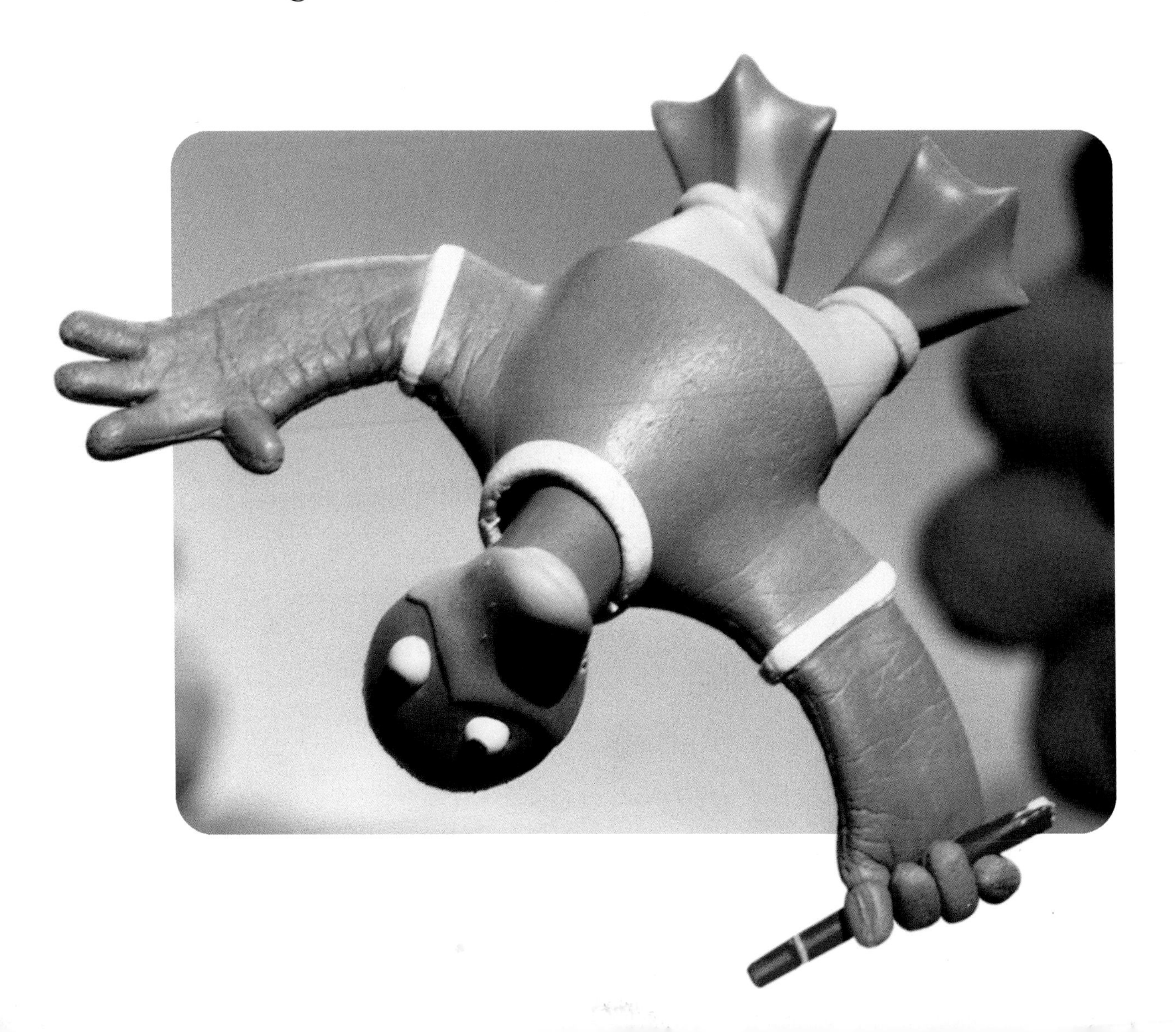

Dr Atticus plunged into the water where, at last, he woke up. He backpaddled out, then trotted over to Derek. He picked up the fishing rod and began to make a splint.

'What are you doing?' Derek quacked.

'Don't worry. I'm a doctor.'

'No, you're not. You're wearing pyjamas.'

'I'm a doctor pretending to be a patient,' Dr Atticus explained. He tied the splint to Derek's wing, then phoned for an ambulance. After that, he was so exhausted he fell asleep again.

‘Ooh, my wing hurts,’ said Derek, as the Teds lifted him into the ambulance. ‘I’ve just been hit by a hospital bed. I was a sitting duck!’

‘Now, now,’ said Ted. ‘You’ve ’ad a little knock on the ’ead. Our ’ospital beds are very friendly. Never ’it anyone, ’ave they, Ted?’ He winked at his brother.

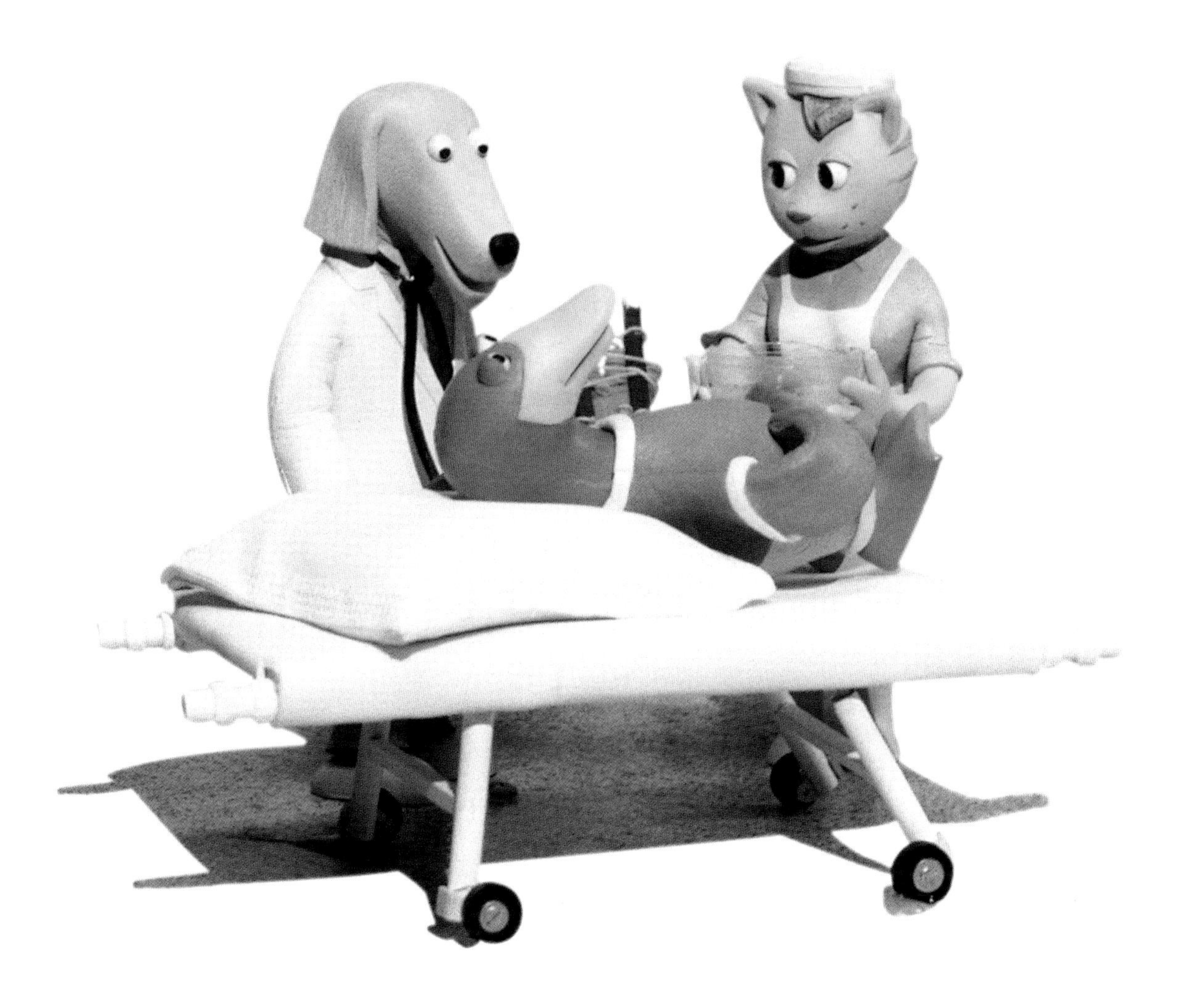

Soon they were back at the hospital. The Teds lifted Derek out of the ambulance and carried him inside on a stretcher. Dr Matthews and Nurse Kitty had a look at Derek's wing.

'We'll have to operate immediately,' said Dr Matthews.

Meanwhile Dr Atticus woke up, just as a police car arrived.

'Everything all right, sir?' asked the policedog.

'Ah, officer. I'm a doctor. I need to get to the hospital immediately. I'm needed for an operation.'

'Doctors don't wear pyjamas, sir.'

'No, I'm a doctor *pretending* to be a patient. My bed ran away with me, crashed into a duck and then sunk in the pond.'

'I see. Do you have a licence to drive a bed?' asked the policedog. 'Perhaps you'd better come with us,' he said, opening the door of the police car.

The operation theatre was being prepared; instruments were cleaned, masks and gowns tied, surgical gloves put on.

'Scalpel!' Sally ordered.

'Scalpel,' Kitty echoed.

'Anaesthetic!' Sally ordered.

There was no reply.

'ANAESTHETIC!' Sally ordered again.

But there was no anaesthetic, because there was no Dr Atticus.

'Oh dear, oh dear, oh dear,' moaned Dr Atticus, sitting in the prison cell. 'This is all my fault for being so lazy.'

Herman Hare, who shared the cell, played a tune on his harmonica to cheer Dr Atticus up, but instead it sent him to sleep again. In fact, he fell off the bed. Herman called for the policedog.

'What's the matter?'

'It's this tortoise.' said Herman. 'I think he needs a doctor.'

Soon the Teds were driving to the police station. Then, having collected Dr Atticus, they returned to Hilltop.

'What's the matter with him?' Ted asked.

'You know how lazy 'e is. Probably collapsed from too much sleep.'

The two Teds laughed.

In the back of the ambulance, Dr Atticus heard what they were saying and felt even more miserable. And that's when he decided he wasn't going to be The Laziest Doctor in the World any more.

As soon as they arrived at Hilltop, Dr Atticus burst out of the ambulance, and shot into the hospital. The Teds looked on in astonishment.

'Was that Dr Atticus?'

'Naw! Tortoises can't run like that.'

But he *was* running like that, straight down the corridor.

Maurice Mosquito was so surprised he pricked his paper cup with his nose.

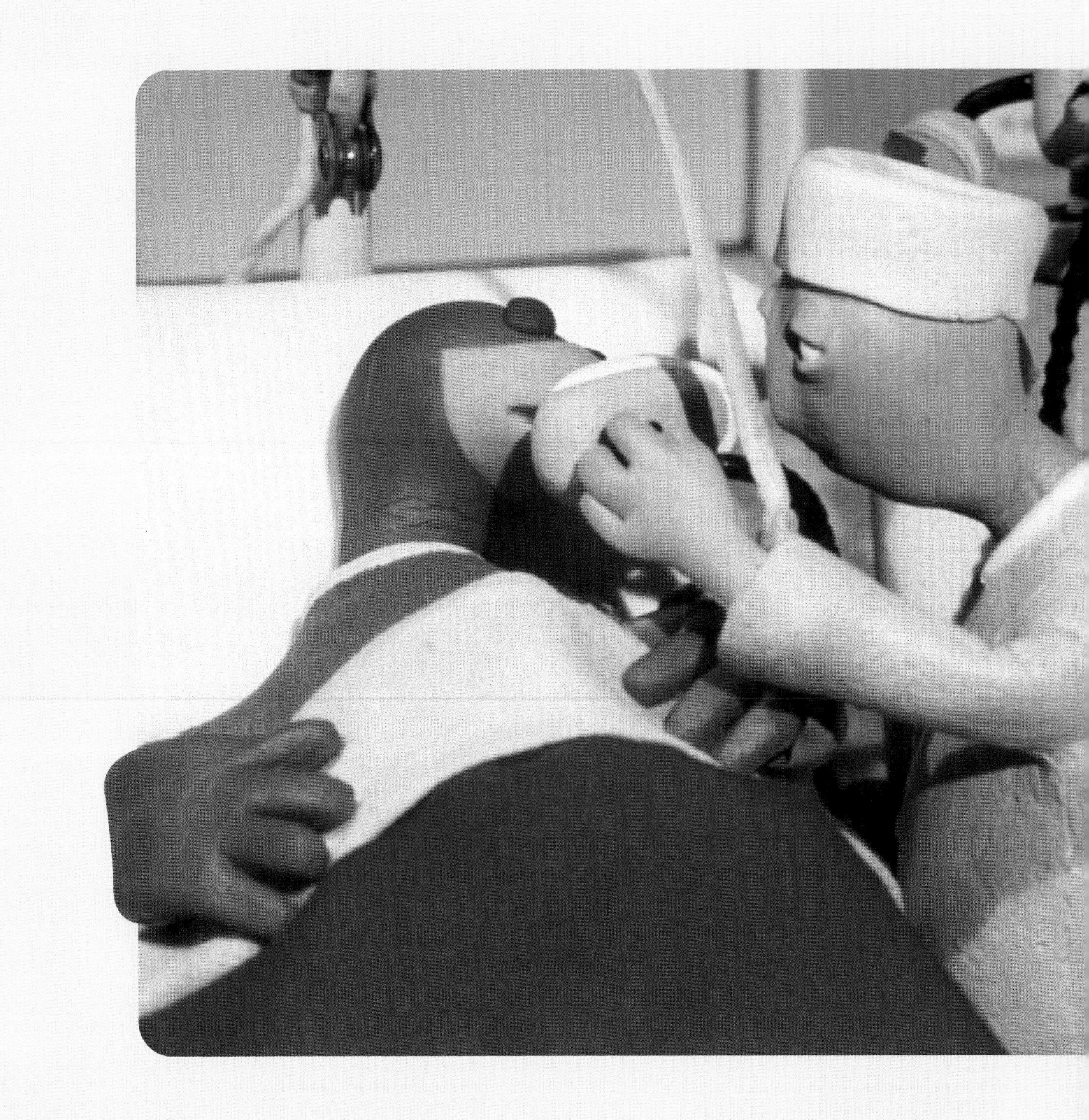

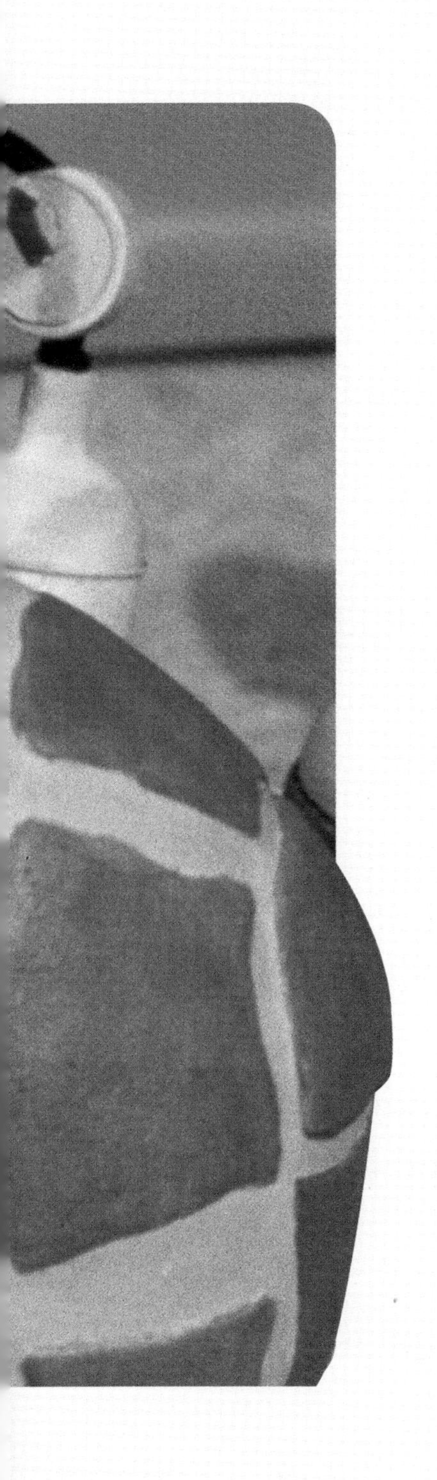

Picking up a white coat and mask, Dr Atticus leapt onto a trolley and sailed through the doors of the operating theatre. Within seconds he was sitting beside Derek Duck.

'Right, let's get on with it. We haven't got all day,' he said. 'Is the patient ready? Surgeon Sally?'

'Who are you?' asked Sally.

'Dr Atticus, of course. And I've got a patient to attend to.'

'Well,' said Sally, amazed. 'In that case, let's begin. Administer anaesthetic.'

'Administering anaesthetic!' Dr Atticus exclaimed triumphantly.

An hour later, the Teds wheeled Derek into the ward.

'I'm glad 'e's stopped quacking on about 'ospital beds 'itting 'im,' whispered Ted.

Then the other Ted asked Derek if he was comfortable.

'Oh yes, thanks. A very comfortable hospital bed. And do you know, it hasn't tried to hit me once!'

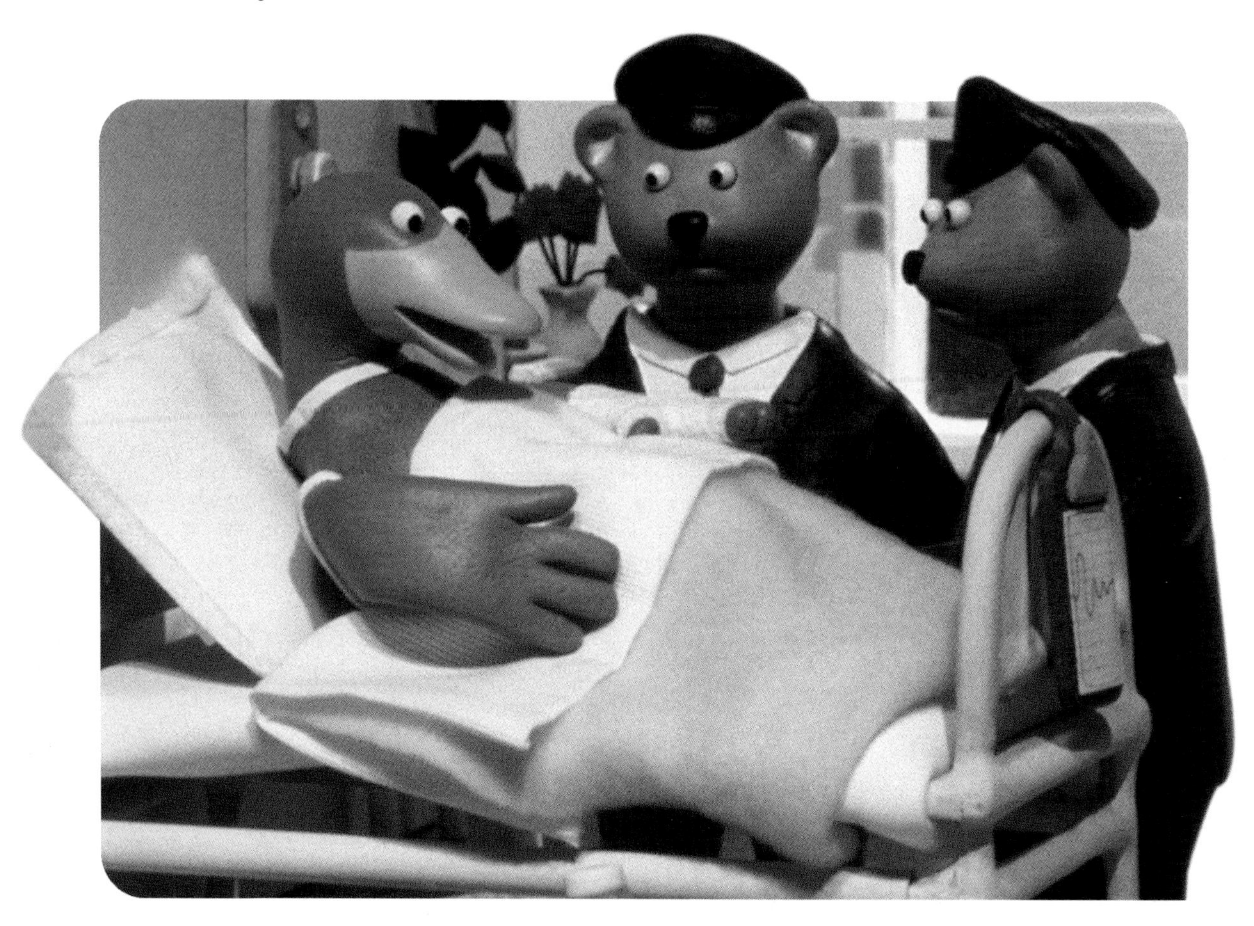

Now that Derek was feeling better, the staff got ready for the great wheelchair race.

They set off. Surgeon Sally took the lead in a yellow sporty number, followed by the lab mice and Dr Matthews.

They zoomed down corridors, sped through the casualty ward, and whizzed round and round the operating table.

Then, as they came to the last lap, a new wheelchair suddenly came into view. It whooshed past Dr Matthews, the lab mice and, with an extra spurt of oxygen, crossed the finishing line just ahead of Surgeon Sally.

The visitors and patients all cheered.

'It's Dr Atticus!' cried the staff. 'Dr Atticus! You've won!'

But Dr Atticus didn't hear. He'd fallen asleep again.